NFL SUPERSTARS
TIKI AND RONDE BARBER

with **ROBERT BURLEIGH**

TEAMMATES

Illustrated by **BARRY ROOT**

A PAULA WISEMAN BOOK

Simon & Schuster Books for Young Readers

NEW YORK LONDON TORONTO SYDNEY

For AJ and Chason—T. B.

To my three Roses—R. B.

To Coach Dwight and the New City All-Stars—B. B.

For Benjamin—B. R.

Acknowledgments

The authors and publisher gratefully acknowledge
Mark Lepselter for his help in making this book.
The illustrator would like to thank Brandon Fortna and also Rem and
Tucker Tshudy and Sam Root for their help with the photo shoot.

SIMON & SCHUSTER BOOKS FOR YOUNG READERS

An imprint of Simon & Schuster Children's Publishing Division

1230 Avenue of the Americas, New York, New York 10020

Text copyright © 2006 by Tiki Barber and Ronde Barber

Illustrations copyright © 2006 by Barry Root

SIMON & SCHUSTER BOOKS FOR YOUNG READERS is a trademark of Simon & Schuster, Inc.

Book design by Einav Aviram

The text for this book is set in Meridien.

The illustrations for this book are rendered in watercolor and gouache.

Manufactured in the United States of America

10 9 8 7 6 5 4 3 2 1

Library of Congress Cataloging-in-Publication Data

Barber, Tiki, 1975–

Teammates / Tiki and Ronde Barber with Robert Burleigh ; illustrated by Barry Root.—1st ed.

p. cm.

"A Paula Wiseman Book."

Summary: "A story of teamwork and perseverance based on the childhood of National Football League stars and
twin brothers Tiki and Ronde Barber"—Provided by publisher.

ISBN-13: 978-1-4169-2489-0

ISBN-10: 1-4169-2489-2

1. Barber, Tiki, 1975– —Juvenile literature. 2. Barber, Ronde, 1975– —Juvenile literature. 3. Football players—
United States—Biography—Juvenile literature. 4. Brothers—United States—Biography—Juvenile literature.
I. Barber, Ronde, 1975– II. Burleigh, Robert. III. Root, Barry, ill. IV. Title.

GV939.A1B3646 2006

796.332092'2—dc22

2005030867

First there was daylight—then there wasn't.

The hole in the line opened and closed that quickly. Smack! Tiki saw the football fly into the air at the same moment he felt his feet go out from under him.

"Fumble!"

"Get it!"

Tiki lay on his side, helplessly watching the squirming mass of arms and legs five yards away. The referee was poking under and peeling off the bodies. Ronde was the next-to-last player at the bottom of the pile.

Maybe? But no. The Vikings had lost the ball on a fumble—for the third time. Yes, it was only a preseason practice game. Still, it was against the Vikings' archrivals, the Knights.

Tiki, head bent, shuffled off the field, wishing he could just plain disappear. He stared down at his two hands. *What gives? I've always carried the ball this way before.*

After the game the twins were waiting for their mother to pick them up. Along with Coach Mike, they walked toward the practice field gate. They sat on a bench by the fence.

Ronde tried to cheer his brother up. "It's okay, Tiki. Mistakes happen."

Coach Mike interrupted. "Mistakes *do* happen. But you can make them happen less often if you . . ." The coach paused, searching for the right words.

"Practice!" Tiki jumped in.

The coach smiled. "Have you heard the old saying: 'Practice makes perfect'?"

The twins smiled back and nodded. Who hadn't heard that one?

"Well, it's not exactly true."

Was this some kind of joke?

"If you're not practicing the right way, you're just practicing your bad habits."

"Huh?"

Coach Mike held the football in front of him with one hand. "If you practice carrying a football like this, you'll never really get good because it is the wrong way to carry the ball."

Then Coach Mike went on. "See: four contact points. One: your fingers around the tip. Two: the other tip in your armpit. Three: one side of the ball against your forearm. Four: the other side against your chest. Try knocking it out," he said.

Tiki and Ronde took turns trying—but no luck. "One, two, three, four contact points," the coach repeated. "You do it." He handed the football to Tiki.

A car horn sounded. The twins waved and scrambled toward their mother's car, with Tiki carrying the football firmly tucked in his arm.

"Hi, Mike!"

"Hi, Mrs. Barber. We were just talking about the right way to carry a football."

Mrs. Barber laughed. "Good. Because we have to carry some boxes of dishes tonight from the pantry to a closet. And I don't want anything dropped!"

In the lunchroom on Monday, Tiki was the last to arrive at the table where several of the football players sat. But something was strange. When Tiki sat down, all the excited talking seemed to stop. Zip.

There was an awkward silence. Tiki glanced at Ronde, who looked away. Slowly the table emptied.

"See you at practice."

At last, Tiki sat alone with Ronde. "What were you guys talking about?"

"Oh." Ronde eyed his half-eaten plate of food. "Nothing."

"Come on. Tell me."

Ronde paused. Then in a quiet voice he said, "Jason and some of the other guys think you should block more and carry the ball less. They think your fumbles are hurting our chances."

Suddenly Tiki's hot dog didn't taste so good.

"And what'd you say?"

"Well, I . . ." Ronde gulped.

"What's that supposed to mean?"

"Tiki, you're our best runner. But maybe . . ."

The bell rang. Tiki took the last bite of his hot dog. The twins headed for the door.

"See you after school in the fort," Tiki called out as Ronde waved and raced up the stairs two steps at a time.

The fort was in a vacant lot. Tiki and Ronde had built it using some old barrels and a few weathered wood planks. Surrounded by tall weeds, it was a perfect hiding place. When a car passed, it seemed far, far away.

This afternoon Ronde had brought their special book. It was really a scrapbook. A big photo of a football was pasted on the cover. Inside the football Ronde and Tiki had each drawn his face with his number beneath it. The scrapbook itself was filled with football players' pictures, facts, and records.

Tiki sat glumly, his mind still on his teammates' words, while his brother flipped the book's pages. Ronde's head bobbed up and down, searching for interesting facts.

"Question: Who's kicked the most career field goals?"

"That's a snap," Tiki answered. "George Blanda. The guy played forever."

Ronde turned more pages. "You think you're so cool? Try this. Walter Payton scored the most career rushing touchdowns. But who's second?"

Tiki thought for a moment. "John Riggins. No, Franco Harris."

"You're wrong twice. Give up?"

"Let's hear it."

"Jim Brown. 106 to Walter's 110."

Suddenly Ronde stopped. He held up a loose sheet containing a picture with a caption underneath it. "Check this out. Some inventor is trying to make a tackling machine."

He handed the picture to Tiki and went on. "It's weird looking. The padded arms try to knock the ball away too. It's supposed to help practice against fumbling."

"It's too complicated. It looks dumb. It won't work."

Ronde studied the picture again, more intently. "Hey." He looked at his brother. "I've got an idea. A better idea!"

"Yo."

"You'll see. It's a surprise. We start tomorrow morning. You game?"

Tiki rolled his eyes. What was this all about? But he and Ronde always did stuff together. "Okay" was all he said. "Whatever."

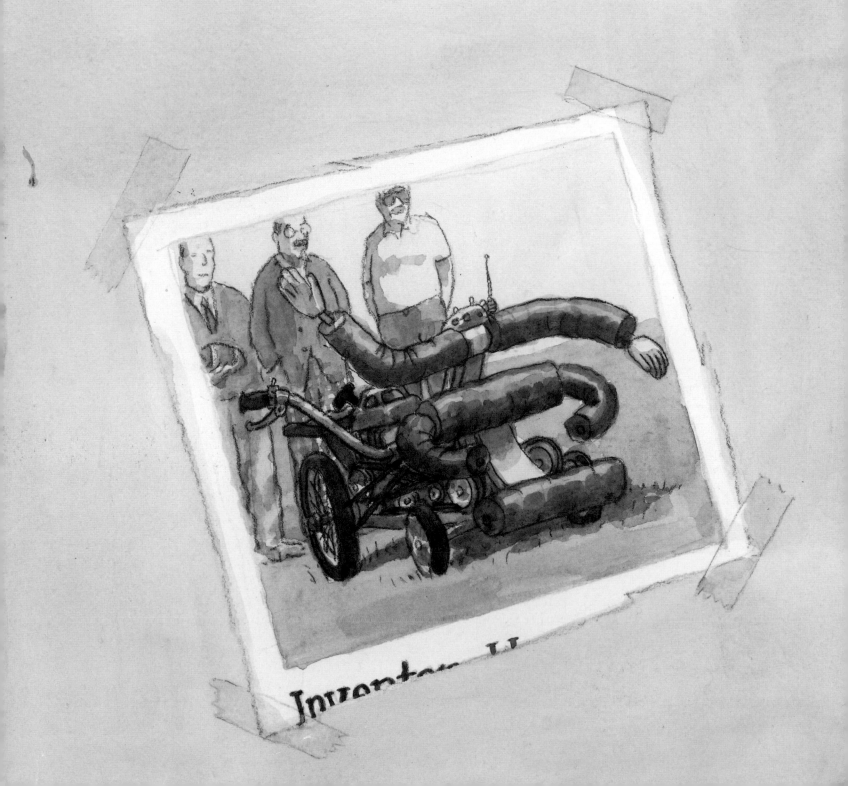

The next morning Tiki and Ronde rode their bicycles in the pale early light. Ronde led the way. Turning into the park, he stopped at the edge of the golf course, got off his bike, and took two helmets and a football from a big bag attached to his handlebars.

"Here." He handed Tiki a helmet. Next he placed two long sticks on the ground to mark off a kind of narrow runway. "Now," he said, flipping Tiki the football, "try to get through a *human* tackling machine."

"Easy." Tiki caught the ball and walked backward. Then he spun around and darted forward, trying to race past Ronde while still staying between the sticks.

Not so fast! Ronde tackled his brother and with a free hand slapped hard at the football. The ball, loosely gripped, popped out of Tiki's arms and dribbled off to one side.

"Again." This time Tiki barreled straight ahead. Ronde ducked underneath and came up with two hands and ripped the football loose. Two-nothing.

It went on like this for a while. Sometimes Tiki and the ball got through, sometimes not. Yet he was beginning to understand. One, two, three, four.

Both boys were gasping for breath. Ronde was having a harder time loosening the ball. They heard a clock chime from a distant tower. "Time to cut. Tomorrow morning?"

"You're on, Bro."

The days passed; hot Indian summer gave way to the cool days of fall. But some things stayed the same.

Tiki and Ronde studied hard each night. "Homework first," their mother always said. And they liked to read. Tiki especially liked books about space flights and astronauts. Ronde loved adventure stories. But the twins also kept up their secret "Morning Practice Club."

And the Vikings started to win.

They won their first game with a strong second-half comeback. They won their second game in a romp. They won number three and then number four. The team was coming together.

Tiki's game was improving too. In the fifth game (another Vikings victory) he was blindsided and dragged to the ground with a hard tackle. But he held on to the ball.

Coach Mike took notice. Tiki no longer waved the ball in the air, or tried to palm it like a loaf of bread, or pushed it out in front as he raced downfield. "Your brother's more than just a *runner* now," the coach remarked to Ronde. "He's a ball carrier. Our go-to guy."

"Yes," Ronde answered the coach. "Tiki's on a roll."

"It's called *confidence*," Coach Mike replied while still watching the action on the field. "And every good football player has it."

Ronde glanced sideways at Tiki and gave a nod that only Tiki could see. Tiki felt stronger than ever. He felt like he was the man!

After a while the secret Morning Practice Club had a new member. Paco was bent over, hands on knees, breathing hard. "So that's it," he exclaimed. "You guys do this extra stuff. When all along I thought you were 'naturals.' And now I find out that—"

Ronde broke in: "Hey, less talk. A few more turns and we're done."

With two tacklers it was much more difficult. Sometimes Tiki got away from Ronde, only to run into Paco, who held Tiki up as Ronde dove at the ball. Sometimes Paco and Ronde hit Tiki at the same time, both swatting the ball. But Tiki held on.

"I should call Paco 'Meat' and you 'Grinder,'" Tiki joked to his brother.

The boys sat on the grass. Saturday was another big game—against the Knights. "They don't just tackle *you*," Ronde said. "They tackle the ball."

"You nervous, Tik?" Paco asked.

"Like coach says: 'Keep the faith.' And I will."

"Tiki nervous?" Ronde answered Paco confidently. "He shakes off any jitters by remembering what coach said: one, two, three, four."

The three friends laughed and clapped high fives. They hopped on their bikes and headed off to school.

Game day—and what a game it was!
Back and forth, up and down, seesaw.
Just like that, the two teams battled through three quarters. First the Vikings,
then the Knights. Then the Vikings, then the Knights.

First quarter: 7-7.
Halftime: 14-14.
Third quarter: 21-21.

Then, with five minutes left and the game still tied, the Vikings offense raced onto the field. Coach Mike's words echoed in their ears: "Hold on to the football" (he had looked hard at Tiki when he said this), "eat up the clock," and "score the game winner."

The Vikings huddled. Across the line of scrimmage the Knights were shouting, "Turnover! Turnover!"

But Tiki heard none of it. He only heard Jason calling his number. He only heard the beating of his own heart. He wanted the ball, and he wasn't going to give it up. He wanted the ball—and he got it. Again and again.

Tiki, with knees high, spun inside the left tackle.
He slammed into and over a linebacker up the middle.
He sprinted around a defensive end.
He plowed straight ahead, behind Ronde, over Paco at right guard.
Three yards, seven yards, five yards, eight yards.
Again and again.

Everywhere he ran, he found a swarm of tacklers. Arms swung out, hands grabbed, fingers clawed at the football.

But Tiki never let go. Somewhere deep inside him a voice said simply, *This ball is mine, mine.*

Yards piled up. Seconds became minutes. Tick-tick. Tick-tick.

The clock was winding down. In the huddle Paco slapped Tiki on the shoulder pads and shouted, "You're doing it, Velcro!" as Ronde sighed, "Yeah!"

On the final play three Knights tackled Tiki, grabbing with all their strength at the ball. But no use. Tiki, head down and clasping the ball to his chest, drove ahead. He struggled free and dove, pushing hard. The game-ending horn sounded.

Tiki, still clutching the football, looked from the pileup to see Ronde grinning.

"You can let go now, Bro. You held on for us. And you scored. Game's over!"
Tiki bounced to his feet and tossed the ball to Ronde. The Vikings were shouting, jumping, and waving.

Ronde laughed out loud. "But now we can let it go," he called out.

Then he flung the football as high as he could into the air. *Victory!*